CU00868723

Once Upon A Place

Edited and introduced by Miranda Walker 2017

An Anthology by the Cheltenham Festivals'
Beyond Words Group at Gloucestershire
Hospital Education Service

Published by Cheltenham Festivals, 2017
Copyright © Cheltenham Festivals 2017

First published in the UK in 2017 by Cheltenham Festivals
109 Bath Road, Cheltenham, Gloucestershire, GL53 7LS

www.cheltenhamfestivals.com

Typeset and cover design by Emma Evans
Cover illustration by Luke Instone-Hall
Printed in Gloucestershire by StroudPrint

Cheltenham Festivals is a registered charity no. 251765

ISBN: 978-0-9954749-1-8

CHELTENHAM
Festivals

Cheltenham Festivals is the charitable organisation comprised of the internationally acclaimed Jazz, Science, Music and Literature Festivals. Through cutting-edge and creative programming, Cheltenham's four inspirational festivals have been at the forefront of the UK's cultural scene since the inaugural Music Festival in 1945.

By championing the best emerging talent, celebrating the work of established artists and commissioning unique and surprising performances, Cheltenham Festivals enriches the cultural lives of its audiences.

An extensive outreach programme with schools and local communities exists year-round to extend the impact of the Festivals and to inspire and empower new audiences.
www.cheltenhamfestivals.com

Gloucestershire Hospital Education Service (GHES) is a registered PRU (Pupil Referral Unit) commissioned by Gloucestershire County Council. The aim of the service is to address inclusion and reintegration issues specific to young people with medical needs; making it possible for a child to have a seamless transition between hospital, home and school. We provide education for all Gloucestershire pupils who are unable to attend school for medical reasons whether mental ill health or physical ill health. We provide this education through our Gloucestershire Royal Hospital (GRH) Schoolroom and our Outpatient Team. GHES also provides support and education to school-aged parents and pregnant schoolgirls. GHES generally support approximately 600 pupils each academic year in hospital and in pupil's homes. GHES works in partnership with pupils' registered schools to provide a flexible and balanced curriculum, which meets the need of each child while they are out of school as well as assisting in a smooth transition back to school.
www.gloucestershire.gov.uk/ghes

About Beyond Words

Cheltenham Festivals and Gloucestershire Hospital Education Service designed **Beyond Words** to support young people to achieve, thrive and reach their potential through the arts despite their medical needs.
Beyond Words was created to improve both students' writing and their well-being, which go hand in hand. Forming part of the students' extra-curricular enrichment programme, groups of students met together in inspiring spaces to discuss, share, laugh and write over a series of months.

Digital versions of the workshops, made possible by GHES staff, made the experience accessible to students who were unable to attend in person either following discharge from hospital or because they are being cared for in the community. These sessions were supported by the GHES Outpatient Team who provide tuition to these young people in their homes or alternative venues.
Inpatients at Gloucester Royal Hospital were also included through a workshop in the Schoolroom.

Beyond Words is richer through collaboration with the University of Gloucestershire. Illustration undergraduates responded to the brief for the front cover art work and Photography students did the same for the supporting imagery. The GHES students became the clients, visiting the University twice to work alongside the undergraduates.

Miranda Walker was the writer for the project this year. An accomplished author and writer for stage, TV and radio, Miranda brought all of this skill and experience to the workshops. Miranda took joy in fostering a love of writing in the students; they responded unreservedly to her warmth and commitment.

The students were co-producers throughout: for the anthology they wrote the content; selected the cover art work and supporting photography; influenced the layout; and saw the book coming off the printing press. In addition, they planned the launch event at Waterstones and will present their work as published authors at The Times and The Sunday Times Cheltenham Literature Festival in October 2017.

We are proud to present this anthology which celebrates the work produced by students during the project. This exciting collaboration has resulted in much more than a book. The benefits of this project have been immense, and in some cases, life-changing.
We are immensely grateful to St.James's Place Foundation for making **Beyond Words** possible.

Ali Mawle
Director of Education, Cheltenham Festivals
Annalise Price-Thomas
Head of Gloucestershire Hospital Education Service
Kathy Heathfield
GHES Beyond Words Project Co-ordinator & GHES English Lead Teacher

Students' Comments

"I have evolved as a writer and my parents have noticed a more confident me. Everyone on the project has been great company and I've made some great friends."

Jack McCune

"I write a lot more now. I actually want to write rather than it being a chore."

Sam Predgen-Lay

"I realise that I'm better at writing than I thought I was!"

Alex Cassie

"It's been good – not just because of the writing but I'm getting out and seeing people similar to my age and whose lives are not going according to plan."

Jess Ephgrave

"It's had a really positive impact: I'm more confident, I've been writing more and got more of a positive attitude. I can now see myself writing as a career."

Louis Maxted

"I've met people with similar issues – it has been so nice to get involved and be part of something. It has reminded me that I can do things. I'm looking forward to speaking at the Cheltenham Literature Festival."

Lucy White

INTRODUCTION

It has been an absolute privilege to be
Writer-in-Residence for the **Beyond Words**
project. As my year in the role draws to a close, I
am glowing with pride for our truly wonderful writers.
All of them are experiencing a bump in the road.
They are not well enough to attend school and
they are constantly managing their illnesses. Some
are in pain or uncomfortable and many experience
crushing tiredness or anxiety, all of which impact
on their concentration and learning. They miss
their friends, and all too often this leads to feelings
of isolation and a lack of confidence. The extent of
their life experience is curtailed, so it is common to
feel left behind.

Our first workshop session took place at Museum
in the Park. Our writers were apprehensive, and as
each took their seat, the tension was evident. We
began in the usual way, with me telling the group
a little bit about myself and my writing. But this
time I included a usually glossed over part of the
story – that I began writing during a bump in the
road too, when a period of illness suddenly took
my life in a different direction.

I was a long-term stealth, under-the-radar writer,
filling notebooks that were just for me. But now,
I stumbled across a way to still participate in the
world from which I felt I had disappeared. I had
a writing voice that I could project. Out there.
Without me. It could cut through and represent
until I could be present again.

I didn't know then that my life would forever
be changed, not by the illness as feared, but by

the writing... I haven't put that voice away since, although thankfully, we are now side-by-side in the world together.

With purpose and sincerity, the group embraced every writing exercise, from the first to the last. We wrote together in a series of workshops, taking inspiration from the amazing locations in which we met, including the beautiful Manor By the Lake, the atmospheric Sudely Castle and the exciting Everyman Theatre. The writers then diligently developed their own work at home, with growing confidence and passion. We introduced them to the tools and techniques of a writer... now they wield them independently with zeal and creativity. We hope you might be inspired by the work in this book to try some of our writing exercises, which appear at the end.
During this project, our writers have grown in conviction. They have bravely written from the heart. They have let themselves be inspired and they have been an inspiration. We have talked and laughed a lot. And I will miss them.
Thank you to everyone involved in **Beyond Words**. Writers – I wish you the very best for your own next chapter. Remember it is often only a page turn away.

Miranda Walker

www.mirandawalker.co.uk
Twitter: @Miranda_W

CONTENTS

1. Beyond Words – Louis Maxted

3. Moral Compass

5. Defining – Jess Ephgrave
7. The Ignorant – Sam Predgen-Lay
9. Simple – Jess Ephgrave
11. Hustle – Louis Maxted
12. A True Thief – Sam Predgen-Lay
17. WHY – Jess Ephgrave

19. Bonds That Tie

21. Coming Home – Lucy White
23. The Whirring of Motors – Sam Predgen-Lay
27. She Was The Girl – Jess Ephgrave
28. Archer's Point of View – Charlotte Lumsdon
33. For Once – Charlotte Lumsdon

35. All Creatures Great and Small

36. Man's Best Friend – Jack McCune
37. Creation Through the Power of Bears –
Alex Cassie
38. Reborn – Jack McCune
41. Where And When – Lauren Arnold

47. Lasting Legacies

49. Beacon – Alex Cassie
50. Balor – Louis Maxted
51. Battle – Alex Cassie
52. Death in 500 Words – Jack McCune
55. The Room – Jess Ephgrave

57. Horikawa Ebisu Shrine – Sam Predgen-Lay
59. Watching – Jess Ephgrave
60. Silver Chalice – Jack McCune

65. On the Dark Side

66. Along the Road – Alex Cassie
67. SLEEP – Jess Ephgrave
69. Smoke – Alex Cassie
71. In Seconds – Keisha Herbert-Valentine

73. Darker Still

75. In My Room – Jack McCune
77. Broken and Weak – Lucy White
79. Countdown – Alex Cassie
80. Dark Smiles – Lucy White
83. Into the Fire – Louis Maxted

85. Joking Hazard

86. Office – Alex Cassie
87. A Lesson in Trickery – Louis Maxted
89. Twisted Proverbs – Jack McCune

93. About Our Lead Authors

97. Your Turn
Featuring the ideas of Hannah Dingle

Beyond Words

Once upon a place in Cheltenham town on a brisk Tuesday morning, six would be authors gather to engage in heartfelt dialogues about literature; quickly gaining an increasing amount of respect for one another while also swiftly forging unyielding friendships that truly are...
Beyond Words.

Louis Maxted

Moral Compass

Defining

I don't want being ill to define me but in so many ways it does. It controls what I do. It stops me seeing my friends, going out, playing sport, doing "normal" teenage things. It stops me doing things I love like playing music and spending time outdoors. My escape is often reading but I can't always do that... I even miss going to school which is something I never thought I would say.

But I am also happy for what being ill has done to me. It has changed the way I look at life. I have learned to love the small things and to appreciate what I can do so much more. It has taught me that no one's life is perfect; there is something making it hard whether that is being ill or worrying about work, being scared of something or worrying about someone else.

But in our world, in our strive for the "perfect" life, there has to be something that defines you and makes you who you are. I would love for what defines me to be a grand thing, maybe one day that will come, but for now I will take what's given and make the most of it. Being ill defines me and I can live with that.

Jess Ephgrave

5

The Ignorant

"The ignorant are ignorant of their ignorance."
They would rather die than admit they were wrong,
Throwing their insults back and forth,
Like a proverbial game of Ping-Pong.

They sit behind their flat-screen castles,
Catapulting their opinions across the world,
Battling with swords made from words,
Their hatred fully unfurled.

Their arguments beamed throughout the globe,
A spectacle for everyone to watch,
They act like they've risen above us all,
Yet they have not even moved but a notch.

But they lead the sheep with their hollow promises,
Most people don't have clue,
That they are being guided right off the edge,
But you're not like them… are you?

Quote: Peter Baskerville

Sam Predgen-Lay

Simple   A simple sad soul

All alone and forgotten

Never remembered

Jess Ephgrave

Hustle

WWE is not my guilty pleasure; I will never be ashamed to admit that pro wrestling is one of the few things that I can always enjoy no matter how anxious, depressed or ill I feel. The compelling storylines and characters coupled with insane feats of human endurance and athleticism will always be something of which I am in awe...

I am proud to admit that Shawn Michaels sends chills up and down my spine with his "Sweet Chin Music." I am proud to admit that when the Undertaker's music plays, I get goose bumps. Every RKO, Stunner, Sharpshooter, Codebreaker, Pedigree, Crossface, Piledriver, Jackhammer and Power-Bomb has me jumping out of my seat!

Wrestling can be silly or goofy at times, but it can also be powerful and affect the viewer's emotions in the same way any good film or TV performance should. The scripted and predetermined nature of wrestling exists to create intriguing stories with complex character dynamics, building up to one big FEEL GOOD moment when the underdog finally captures the world title.

(And as someone who has trained professionally to become a wrestler, I can tell you that it hurts... a lot.)

Louis Maxted

A True Thief

This city is dying. For most, this brings great sadness
and fear, but not me. Not a thief. A dying city is a
thief's paradise. We already know how to live on
little, how to survive with not a coin to your name.
You become cunning and learn that you can't just
think outside the box. You need to manipulate the
box. After a while you can manipulate people from
the shadows. Like sending a threatening letter to an
anxious nobleman so that the guards who protect
the vault are tasked with guarding him. Simple things
like this aren't thought of by a normal bystander but
thought of by a brain perfectly moulded for the job.
A true thief.

One day I was talking to Lenora, my informant
who tells me about rumours and information she
has overheard. She had contacted me and sounded
extremely excited so I headed over to see what all the
fuss was about. It turned out that she had eavesdropped
on a few of the city guards talking about a huge pile
of precious gemstones and expensive jewellery soon
to be carted through the city up to the King's keep. I
assumed she would ask for a hefty sum of money for
the information like usual. "
Information costs more than diamonds!" she always
says. However this time she only asked for one thing,
a small necklace. Apparently it had been taken by
one of the guards as a "new tax" and she desired for
it to be returned.

This was an immense operation and even though my abilities and intuition had never failed me, I knew I could not do this alone. Thankfully this depleted city had enough gangs to make a really terrible joke. All I needed to do was slip bits of information to a couple of the gangs and let the inevitable fighting take place. They would skirmish all over the city but if you wanted some huge fights to create a lot of confusion, you would need to give them incentive. I knew that they wouldn't dare let one of the other gangs get the loot. I also knew from past experience that the gangs would forget about the cart packed with gems as soon as the first blood was drawn. The perfect distraction.

It was the day before the convoy entered the city from the harbour. According to Lenora, a cargo ship called the "King's Pride" would sail into the harbour baring gems and exotic materials. The convoy was waiting in unguarded storage as there was nothing yet to steal. However I wasn't here to steal, I was here to tamper with and sabotage the last carriage. Loosen a few screws here and there or weaken the axel. I did both for good measure. Whilst I was there, I checked whether my intel was correct. It turns out that the back of the carts had no windows. Little did they know that this little oversight would be a huge part of my plan.

This was the day. I had previously asked Lenora to do a little snooping and find out who would be driving the loaded cart. She did her job exceptionally as always and provided me with his name and address. I walked up to his tiny apartment and knocked on the door. An equally tiny man in a uniform three sizes too big for him opened the door. I quietly mumbled, "Sorry about this," as I proceeded to punch him in the face. He stood there for a moment before falling comically back into a mirror, which slowly creaked forward into his face. This really wasn't his lucky day. I quickly put on his clothes, which seemed to fit me better than him, and headed over to the harbour.

Trying to avoid conversation and eye contact, I made my way to the cart and boarded. I could faintly see the gems and gold shining less than a metre behind me, but I was far from done. I watched the first cart trundle out of the storage warehouse. I tugged on the rains and promptly followed. As I exited I heard the last cart start moving - I could hear the sound of wood scraping against wood. This was the sound of the axel slowly being worn down as it trundles along. We started off slow but as the front drivers saw the amount of gang members building, they quickened the pace. We were soon in the heart of the city and out of fear the front drivers started going even faster with me following suit.

CRACK! I glimpsed behind me to see the last cart's wheel fly off, hitting an unfortunate gang member in the face. The cart leaned and hit the curb causing it to do an impressive barrel roll before screeching to a halt. As I turned back I saw the opportunity. A fork in the road. A split through the heart of the city. The cart in front of me turned to the right as I veered to the left. Within an instant the front car was lost from view as I started spiralling down the street into the working district. I slowed the cart so not to stand out and turned right into a small alley. The working district was a labyrinth of small alleys and dead ends and unlike me the guards never came down here. It was the perfect place to lay low.

I traversed the labyrinth with ease and soon found myself at the old lumber yard where my own cart lay in wait. Using the time I had gained through the labyrinth and hoping the front cart went all the way to the Keep before noticing, I shovelled all the gems to the other cart. I then paid the woodcutter to destroy the old cart, covering my tracks. After switching into my clothes, I simply drove my cart past guards and civilians all the way to my trove on the outskirts of town, where I unloaded everything. I gazed upon my sweet, shining victory. I had done it. Outsmarted a whole city. Something only I could do.
A true thief.

Sam Predgen-Lay

WHY

Why should pleasing men influence our appearance?

Why should woman have to change themselves for men?

Why should we be forced to explain what we want to wear, too slutty or prude or too threadbare?

What should it matter if we adore shoes or not?

Why should it matter if we're fat or we're thin?

Why should we be told what we can and can't do "That's not ladylike," and "Oh, that's for boys, not you."

Why should it be noteworthy if we have a female PM?

Why should it be shocking if we voice our opinions?

Why should men get all the best jobs?

Why should women be chained to the stove, forced to bear children and suppress their woes?

Why should women need to have kids to be seen as complete?

Why should women work all day and then be expected to run a home as well?

Why should women feel guilty if they can't do it all?

Can you justify or explain why women are still asking these questions today?

Jess Ephgrave

Bonds That Tie

Coming Home. Photograph by Freya Gray

Coming Home

"Dad! DAD!!!" I yelled as I walked through the
flimsy front door.

"Dad?" He wasn't in the kitchen with a beer or
in the living room (a sofa in the kitchen) watching
football.

"Mum?"

I knew she was supposed to be working at the
corner shop, but I'd caught her off work and lying
in bed a number of times.

"I'm here, sweetie," I could hear her voice coming
from the bathroom.
Carefully placing my guitar next to the door, I
walked in and found her lying in an empty bath.

I could smell something awful –

the smell you get under the footbridge down the
street, where some people at my school went at the
weekend.

Her eyelids were drooping; her hands were limp
and dangled on the edges of the bath.

"I'm tired, can you let me sleep, sweetie," she said in a drowsy voice, in a childlike way.

"Mum...
what did you buy this time? I told you not to talk to that man again."

I whispered softly to her, stroking her lifeless fingers. She groaned and turned away.

A loud bang vibrated through the house.

"How much did you make me this time, Mads?"

It was my Dad. He'd just come back from the pub, I guessed.

I could hear his hands rubbing together and the thirst for cash in his harsh voice.

Little did he know that a giant cheque was sitting at the bottom of my rucksack.

Lucy White

22

The Whirring of Motors

I hate that noise.

The whirring of motors as it shuffles about its cell.

I hear it joking and laughing with the other inmates, fooling them into thinking it's their friend.

It avoids me now.

It tried talking to me when I first got in here but I made it very clear that I never wanted to talk to its kind.

They disgust me.

I remember what my father used to tell me; stories about how they were all murderous monsters that were going to destroy humanity.

The news was always showing clips of cyborgs robbing banks or hurting innocent people.

When I looked out of my window I could see the other kids playing with them.

My father wouldn't let me go out and play with them because he said that they would hurt me, so I sat watching them and despised them for forcing me to stay inside and not have fun like the other kids.

The Whirring of Motors. Photograph by Gareth Chamberlain and Al Pitt.

The only time I remember having any fun was when my father took us down to the beach.

We ate chips while swatting away the savage sea-gulls as they pounced on our lunch.

While my father was swimming and my mother was sun bathing, I walked around marvelling at the pretty white rocks laced with fossils.

I picked up the best looking ones and strolled back to our beach tent.

When I got back, my father had packed up everything and told me that we were leaving.

When I queried why we had to leave so soon, he pointed up the beach to a group of cyborgs who were just setting up their tent.

Once again my fun had been stolen by these vile false humans and it was those false humans that got me into this mess.

When I was older and had finished education, I
found a group of like-minded people who also
hated cyborgs.
They told me about their plans to strike back at
them.
I was at my first meeting when I heard the sirens.
They got louder until suddenly the door crashed
open revealing a swat team with guns trained to
our heads.
We all got on the floor and I saw that the police
force had also been infested with cyborgs.

A cyborg held my trial and a cyborg put me in
prison.

It tried to talk to me again today.
It tried to trick me into playing a game with it.

But I won't be tricked.

I know he wants to kill me.
They all want to kill me.
So I will kill them.

I grabbed the pebble from my desk and threw it at
him. It connected with his head with a satisfying thud.
He dropped to the ground as I picked up the
bigger rock.
I smashed it against his skull until all his chips
were shattered into pieces and all went silent.

Later that day they took me into solitary confinement.
I didn't care.
I had finally taken my revenge and it felt amazing.
I sat in my cell to enjoy the silence and that's when I
heard it.

The whirring of motors.

Sam Predgen-Lay

She Was The Girl

She was the girl I gave my heart to, the one
who gave me hers.

When I met her she was innocent and perfect
in every single way.

The night she came to me, the night she asked
for help started as the happiest night of my life.

It's funny how just a few seconds can change
your world forever.

No one really knows what happened, well only
me and her.

They gave us a choice to live or to die and of
course we chose to live.

I only realise now that the latter was the better.

The things they made us do for life will forever
haunt my dreams; when she could not take it
anymore she closed her eyes and never truly
woke again.

But it doesn't matter now what happened all
those years ago.

 Even though I still sit here, watching over her,
wishing for time to stop, for the clocks to wind
back so I can erase the things that happened
and start that night again.

Jess Ephgrave

Archer's Point of View

There she is -
Melody St. James, 20 years of age, no living relatives,
total number of two friends.
One of which is a dog.

She is stunningly attractive... and her occupation?
A PI hired by the state attorney Cliff Barnes to look
into the case of the mysterious and infamous bank
robber the press like to call Shadow.

Me.

I sit in a dark corner of Starbucks with Melody's file
—
acquired by my partner in crime and techno geek of
a best friend, Jordan watching her.
Now this may seem totally creepy, but it's needed.

She might be just a girl who never actually graduated
high school, but she's damn good at her job; almost
too good.
On my last heist, me and my team slipped up badly.
We didn't know she had worked out our pattern,
how we chose which bank to hit, or that she had an-
ticipated our next move and knew when and where
we'd hit next.

The cops came and we had to take 37 hostages to get
away; 20 men, 15 women and 2 children.

To call it close would be an understatement.
After that we went into hiding.

Jordan hacked into the state attorney's email account and found records on the recruitment of Miss Melody St. James.

It was hard to find much on her, the girl knew how to cover her tracks, but once we got the basics, I needed this stake out to find out what she knows about us.
So far it looks like she has nothing, but it's only a matter of time.
She needs a distraction; I smirk, knowing the perfect thing to take her pretty little mind off of her work.

Melody is in a corner by a window. I walk over to her, then stand there, astounded by her beauty.

Sure, I've seen pretty girls before, but Melody isn't pretty, she's beautiful.
Her grassy green eyes concentrating hard on her laptop, her face perfectly structured with her sloped nose, high cheek bones and defined jaw.

Looking at her up close I can see a faint scar above her perfectly arched left eyebrow.
Her straight, raven-black hair is up in a messy pony tail and as a strand of hair flitters down in her eyes, my fingers itch to tuck it behind her ears.

Stupid Archer, what the hell is wrong with you?

"May I help you?"
She asks, her eyes not moving from her computer
screen.

"Umm... is this seat occupied?"
I gesture to the empty seat across from her.

"No, but the seat you came from looks pretty
comfortable."
She looks up from her computer screen for the first
time…
and nothing, no stutter, no dilation of the eyes.

No signs of her being attracted to me at all.

I don't let it phase me though as I sit in the chair,
look into her eyes and say,
"But this one has a better view..."

She rolls her eyes.

"You know, if you do that too much your eyes will
get stuck at the back of your head?"

She looks up at me with a sickly sweet smile,
"At least then I wouldn't have to look at your face."

I chuckle. She's cute when she's feisty.

"What's your name gorgeous?"

"Gorgeous?" She looks me up and down, and
uninterested, goes back to looking at her computer.

"Well, nice to meet you mystery girl, I'm Archer..."

Charlotte Lumsdon

For Once. Photograph by Gareth Chamberlain.

For Once

The way I saw it, there were only two types of people:
good and bad.
I wasn't interested in either.
I did my job avoiding as much interaction as I
could, then went home to my log cabin in the middle
of the woods by a lake, to be with my husky puppy
called Lobo;
I named him that because it means wolf in Spanish.

But this person intrigued me, I was just as curious
with this person as Lobo was when he found a spider
under the couch.

There was something about this person that even a
blind man could see was special.
No, it wasn't the way his mouth twitched upwards
when he had just made you as red as a tomato by
twisting your words into an innuendo.
Or the way that he could charm you into just about
anything … he could probably even charm you into
robbing a bank!

He was unique, almost mystical.
Yet his free spirit was a drastic contrast to those
ocean blue devoid-of-emotion eyes.

This was strange for me; I don't associate myself
with anyone, yet I wanted to know him.

I needed to figure out this walking enigma.

For once I was interested.

Charlotte Lumsdon

All Creatures Great and Small

Man's Best Friend

A hairy furry face, with innocent loving eyes.

A warm raspy tongue ready to lick you to death with affection.

A mad mind-of-its-own tail, constantly wagging in your presence.

A wet coal black gumdrop nose relentlessly sniffs you.
Hoping to find some hidden treat for his bottomless stomach.

Short dirty brown bristly fur covers his terrier body.
Velvety black ears droop lazily on the sides of his small head.

His mouse-sized paws hook protectively around your leg when he sits on your lap.

A girly squeal escapes him every time you tell him it's walkies.

Or breakfast time.

His panting breath takes up a puffing train rhythm when he barbeques himself in front of the fire.

And when you're down or upset, he will always be there with a hug and a lick.

This is my dog.

The one and only Sid.

Jack McCune

36

Creation Through the Power of Bears

In the beginning there was nothingness and the
eternal bear, until the eternal bear roared.
As he roared, so began the event that forged our
universe, the Bear Bang.

From the great bear's jaws sped forth the galaxies
filled with stars and the masses of matter that would
later form our planets and other celestial bodies, and
slowly, over billions of years, our entire universe.

More than could be imagined was created.

Alex Cassie

Reborn

The golden sand dunes of Egypt rose and fell like
motionless ocean waves over a barren landscape
devoid of life.
It was eerily quiet.
There was no birdsong, and none of the usual
bustling sounds from the distant city of Heliopolis
reached this part of the vast sun-scorched desert.
Tiny grains of powder dry sand lay motionless
beneath the merciless unrelenting rays of the fiery
midday sun.
Not even the wind whistled.
All was quiet as if time had decided to stand still.

In the heart of the desert stood a timeworn ash
grey mesquite tree.
Its tusk-like branches reached out as if desperate to
find water to quench its parched roots. Like with-
ered arms the branches seemed to beg for shelter
from the relentless barrage of heat from the unfor-
giving sun.
Perched on the topmost branches of this wretched
tree was a dowdy looking bird.
Its eyes sealed shut and its head bowed deep into its
chest as it slumbered in the afternoon sun.

The bird's once ruby red feathers where now grey
like the stormiest cloud you could imagine. His
bronze claws, which in days long past had been
fierce weapons, were now chippered, cracked and
appeared to be rusting.
His once magnificent plumage which made pea-
cocks bow their heads in shame now resembled a
moth-eaten tapestry.

Now all animals great and small, savage or timid,
weak or powerful mocked and looked down at what
the vicious jaws of time had done to him.

With a feeble croak the bird opened its eyes. Immediately your attention was diverted from its physical imperfections as it held you transfixed in its gaze.

The ice blue eyes were deep and penetrating and the pupils were as black as night.
No other sentient could claim to have seen as many horrors and wonders as these eyes had witnessed.

As the bird raised its decrepit form off the branch, the toll this took on his waning form was obvious. Sluggishly the shabby creature hobbled across the sun- bleached branch towards what would be its final resting place;
his nest.
Gently the bird lowered itself onto the centre of a self-crafted funeral pyre of cinnamon twigs, myrrh and frankincense.

Gazing around at the surrounding landscape, his home, for the last time, he thought his final thought, 'What a beautiful place it was.'
The bird closed its weary eyes and breathed in the clean, pure air of the unspoilt desert.
Wings raised up to its shoulders, the bird spread them out wide.

Suddenly, with a roar that rivalled an erupting volcano, the bird burst into a ball of fierce writhing, hungry, amber flames.

This was an unnatural fire.

The flames danced as if alive as they coiled around the bird like a boa constrictor. They consumed the fragile body like a ravenous monster.

Then no sooner had it began, the flames were extinguished.

The magic was over.

The new Phoenix rose up from the ashes of its predecessor;
ready to begin its new life.

Its blood red feathers stood out in drastic contrast to the pale yellow sand of the desert surrounding it.

Its hooked bronze talons where deadly scimitars of death once again. Sprouting out from behind it was a breath-taking display of strikingly vibrant plumage. The golden feathers radiated beauty that rivalled the light from the sun while the silver feathers surpassed the brightest stars.

Then there where the eyes, which at first glance were seemingly unchanged.
They were still as blue ice from the heart of the Antarctic and the pupils remained as black as a starless night.
The only difference was that this pair of eyes were young, fresh and determined.
Ready to see what the trials of the world had to offer.

The Phoenix spread his new pair of wings out wide. Strong and muscular once again, ready for a lifetime of flying.

With an almighty leap the Phoenix took flight and rose majestically into the air, heading straight toward the horizon, ready to begin again.

He had been reborn.

Jack McCune

Where and When

The leaves crinkled under the intruder's feet, the trees creating the only path leading them further into the maze in which only animals had set foot until now.

The branches created a canopy blocking out all but specks of sunlight, yet the forest still had a calming, warm glow resonating from seemingly nowhere.
Even with the apparent lack of sun, the plants were still growing better than most he had seen.

Something about this place was unnerving, whether it was the impossibility of the plants, the glow of the forest, the seeming lack of life (even when he could hear the
pitter-patter of paws running along next to him), or the grandeur of the place making him feel tiny compared to the trees; much like how he had felt in cathedrals, or mansions with the towering ceilings.
Something was off.
Yet he could not help but feel relaxed and at peace.

The stress washed from him the further he was drawn into the heart of the woods, like a siren's call dragging the sailors to their doom... but that wasn't happening now, was it?

Suddenly, a breeze swept through the forest, the leaves crackling in protest.
Yet, like this forest, something was off.
The wind was neither hot nor cold, in fact the human could barely feel it at all while plants were straining against it as if it was a gale.

It was an ominous feeling that washed over the intruder now, the wind feeling more like a warning than a natural occurrence.

Nevertheless, the interruption broke him from his stupor and he realised that the air was fresher than he had ever breathed before.
The suffocating smog was long forgotten, and not even a whisper of the deafening sound of the machines.

How was it possible when this place was only a five minute walk away from the factory?
It was almost as if the atmosphere itself could not pass into this place, the woe of the steam machines never touching this forest.
Something was definitely wrong.

Should he turn back, should he continue?

Curiosity got the best of him and he wandered deeper into the heart of the forest.
"I hope I live long enough to regret this."
Was his only thought before the lights cut out.

"Well, well, well, what do we have here?"
He froze as a voice came from the darkness.
"My, my, the faeries were right, a Human. How long has it been since I have seen one of you in my domain?"
The figure's voice was laced with venom as it started to circle him, almost sizing him up.
"Almost a century I think... Time doesn't really matter to me anymore, but yes, a century sounds about right."

"Who are you?"

His voice wavered, he instantly knew that if he said one wrong thing he would be in a very difficult and possibly life threatening predicament.

"Who am I? You are the intruder here, you have no right to ask questions. Who are you?"

"I asked first."

"What a childish response! Very well, I am the guardian of this place. I protect it from the likes of you and I have done for a very long time. Your kind nearly hunted all of these wonderful creatures to extinction."

He opened his mouth to ask another question, but was cut short by the voice coming from the dark. "Before you ask, I mean humans. Your kind taint, corrupt and destroy, it is all you can do. Now what to do with you? You can't stay here and there is no turning back. I guess I'll just have to get rid of you another way."

The voice sounded female, the intruder thought. Her tone had become threatening and every time he opened his mouth to try to reason with her, she angered or cut him dead.
Maybe it was her voice, or how she remained in the shadow...perhaps it was the way the air stiffened making the atmosphere all the more eerie... whatever it was, his instinct was to run for it, to go back home and never come back here again.

He bolted through the forest, but the trees became dense, the branches clawed at him and any form of light was long gone.

He started to hear low growls and howls.
The sound of fast paws pounding after him, matching the rate of his heartbeat.

Giggles like the tinkle of bells filled the air and felt
like they were drilling into his head;
small flashes of lights here and there blinded him,
his lungs burning until he ran smack bang into
what felt like a tree trunk.

Soon, he lost consciousness.

The intruder's eyes fluttered open, the light
burning but a foreign smell of flowers freshly
covered in dew calming him greatly.

He had awoken in a clearing so quaint and peaceful
compared to his crowded home in the same run
down street.
But it was not long until the painful throbbing in
his head came back, along with memories of the
strange events.

The human was about to panic and run again,
when out of the corner of his eye he saw a rabbit
looking straight at him, greyish blue in colour and
with a small glow emanating from it.
The small creature ran off as soon as he laid eyes
on it, as if it had been waiting for him to notice it.

He scrambled to his feet to follow the creature;
he was barely able to keep up through the twists
and turns of the forest, losing sight of it at times.

He was never close enough to reach it but never far
enough away to lose it forever, as it waited if he fell
too far behind.

After what felt like days, his feet sore, his legs tired, his head aching, they reached what seemed like the edge of the forest.

At last he was free and a sense of euphoria washed over him.
He turned back to thank the creature but it was gone; no footprints, as if it was never there.

He continued forward.
There was a blinding white light and air pushing back, which made him think of wading through water.

Soon there was solid ground under his feet and the sounds of the forest were overpowered by the loud noises rushing past him; he could hear the familiar mumbles of the crowds.

He closed his eyes and drank in the sounds.
He never thought he would be so thankful to be back home.
He had longed for adventure, but he was glad it was over.

Yet when he opened his eyes, he saw something even more bizarre than the forest; strange shaped metal boxes with what looked like people trapped inside rushed past at speeds faster than any horse.

People walked past going about their lives whilst wearing the strangest of clothes. Buildings reached as high as the sky, some seemingly made purely of glass.
People were even talking into little rectangles as if they were a person they knew, while others looked at their rectangles instead of paying attention to their surroundings.

Where was he?
No!
When was he?

Lauren Arnold

Lasting Legacies

Beacon. Photograph by Al Pitt.

Beacon

A radiant aura

shining through the drear

a bright glow in the dark

a beacon of hope

for the helpless

a welcome sight

For the downtrodden.

Alex Cassie

Balor

Upon a mighty cliff in a harsh wasteland, a man stands accompanied by only his shadow and the brisk, bleak winds of winter that blew through his hair.

The black and red colours of his warpaint seem to burst through the ice-cold fog.

His mind is full of the bygone conflicts that have moulded him into the most formidable, fearsome warrior the world has ever seen.

He lives to conquer and destroy all who face him.

His losses only fuel his desire to push his mind and his body further and harder, for war and delivering the coup de grâce!

Louis Maxted

Battle

The thunder of the cavalry charging past brings me
out of my stupor and I look down to see my sword
embedded in a soldier's helmetless head.

I wrench it loose and turn in time to see a
mace-wielding rider rushing towards me and react
fast enough to raise my shield and block a blow that,
had it connected, would have caved in my skull.

He wheels around for another attempt but does
not get a chance as a blue feathered arrow suddenly
sprouts from his neck.

Looking around I now see that as the battle draws to
its conclusion, forces of armoured knights mounted
on barded horses chase after routed Sellswords, and
blue banners stream from raised standards.

Alex Cassie

Death in 500 Words

A.D. 1469

Atop the Octagonal tower a lone guardsman stood watch over the gates of Sudeley Castle.

Clearly embroidered on his mud stained, navy blue cotton tunic was the pale white rose of the House of York.
On his right hip hung a wicked short sword, the edge of the blade was so sharp you simply had to run your finger down it to draw ruby red droplets of blood.
The guard gazed at his only hope should the enemy breach the castle wall.
He so wished that the Quartermaster had issued him with a more reliable blade to defend himself.

The Quartermaster had assured him that this wasn't necessary as he was assigned to the new position of 'gunner'.
He had heard of 'guns', the alleged weapons of 'mass destruction' from fellow soldiers in his regiment. They had frequently bragged about their superiority to current weapons.
But in his opinion the best way to dispatch an enemy soldier was to hack him to ribbons with a two foot long sword!
A bit messy but it got the job done!
These new-fangled weapons would never catch on.

To his left flank was a 'cannon', which he had been assured by his Commanding Officer
"would hold back the vile Lancastrians for sure."

The guard glanced at the cannon beside him, his eyes were still adjusting to its alien shape.
Its long oily black barrel reminded him of an empty tree trunk.
The cold, smooth iron balls that had to be loaded into the belly of the cannon were like overgrown rocks from the caves where the devil lived.

The guard turned his thoughts away from the cannon and returned his watchful eyes to the Lancastrians' camp, which was positioned outside the castle walls. He was keen to carry out his duty which was to blast the souls out of the Lancasters' bodies should they breach the castle gates.

Abruptly, his thoughts were interrupted by the sound of a deep thundering trumpet call. It was the war horn!

The Lancastrians where attacking!

Around the base of the tower he could hear fellow Yorkist soldiers hurrying to mount the wall defences. The clinking and clanking of armour, the rings of swords being drawn and the vicious barks of bully-ing commanders where the only sounds that could be heard.

Many of his friends where down there, manning the defences of the castle walls.

When the battle was over, he looked forward to a game of dice with them and listening to them brag about how many soldiers they had killed.

He hoped that with the cannon on his side he could double anything they tallied!

Suddenly, came an ear drum bursting boom!

His eyes darted frantically, trying to locate the source
of the noise.
But before he could locate the originator, he felt an
almighty force collide with the right side of his head.

Then all went black.

His last thoughts of curiosity dying with him.

Jack McCune

The Room

At first glance it is a simple room, a distant memory of its former life.
The most prominent feature is the holes, the great gaping holes, the holes which pepper the ceiling allowing bright gleaming light to pierce the darkness of the room.

A grand piano stands in the far corner, its keys left uncovered as if it is enticing you in to play and fill the silence with music, beautiful music.

Atop it rests several photographs of a family, stiff and hard, in their Sunday best, providing a temperate view into what their lives were like.

Along the walls hang tapestries faded and worn from people's touch, where they had traced their fingers along the stories they depicted.

Scattered between these are paintings.
Their occupants, like the ones in the photographs, stiff and hard, apart from one depicting two children playing in an orchard.
But even this was just another long forgotten memory.

Thick, velvet curtains frame the windows, covered with heavy oak shutters that block out the view of the untamed gardens below.
Across the wooden floor, a large oriental rug has been spread, now covered in dank, dark patches where the rain has seeped in.

Scattered across the room is an assortment of chairs and tables, the sort of chairs in which you would be expected to only ever sit on the edge and tables with little more purpose than to hold a lamp.

On the furthermost wall is a row of towering shelves, aching under their weight of tattered, sun-kissed books.

Books long denied the chance for their pages to be lovingly turned, transporting their readers to other worlds.

The fireplace, that once was the heart of the room, has become encased in layers of dust and soot, rendering its carving almost indistinguishable and allowing its grand opulence to go unnoticed.

And the air, the air is heavy and cold, filled with a musty, damp scent.
The sort of scent you get in winter when it's too damp for anything to dry properly.
When the rain never seems to cease and the sun never cares to show its face.

Shivering, I turned and closed the door, sealing myself in with my past and its memories.

Jess Ephgrave

Horikawa Ebisu Shrine

As you stride through the busy, bustling streets of
Osaka, your eyes are drawn away from immense
skyscrapers looming over like sentinels, towards the
small and simplistic beauty of the Horikawa Ebisu Shrine.

The first thing that catches the eye is a decrepit,
ancient wooden fence standing either side of a
welcoming bright red torii gate.
When you step through this symbolic gateway, you
feel the fast paced action of the industrial city is left
far behind you, and the tranquil peace of the little
shrine washes over you.

If you take a moment to stop and gaze at the heroic
trees that hold their own against the humungous
buildings which box in this little shrine, you are
captivated by their charm.
Hiding in one of the biggest cities in Japan, the
shrine goes unnoticed by the people of the city as
they go about their business.

Walking towards the little building with the arched
roof rising to a point over the highly decorated
Shinto shrine, you become aware of the numerous
elegant paper lanterns hanging like white and red
moons over the alter.
Each is covered with a flowing mountain stream of
beautiful black kanji symbols.
Most of the day the shrine is quiet with just one little
old monk, whose face is as lined as the paper of the
lanterns above him, tending to the plants and selling
the many charms and trinkets to the occasional visitor.

Most of the shrine's visitors are businessmen who
come before work on a daily baises to wish for
success in their ventures.

These people hardly disturb the peace.

However, on the day of the Toka Ebisu Festival, the peace is shattered like glass by the chanting of many worshippers as they pray for success in business.

The women celebrants arrive traditionally dressed in black kimonos with red and gold sashes, their white makeup
contrasting against their jet black hair.
The shrine is filled with commotion and colour as families pour in to dance around and share a banquet of fantastic food which tastes like ambrosia.

But on this quiet day, the smell of smoke and fumes from the city floods your nose, a direct contrast to the little wooden building in front of you.
The horns and engines of cars in the distance are almost drowned out by the happy tweets and squeaks of different animals that have found sanctuary here.
In this sacred oasis, the vividly coloured birds hop and fly from tree to tree like monkeys in a rainforest.
The sound of the bell slices through the air as it is rung to call the spirits for a blessing.
It is said by some worshippers that you can hear lively danjiri music coming from the shrine when their prayers are answered.
As you cross the threshold of the highly adorned building with the white tiled roof, you smell burning candle wax and see the detailed statues of the gods.

This little Shinto shrine is a huge contrast to the busy, lavish Buddhist temples where tourist flock like magpies to jewels.
Here, the calm relaxes you and when you tread back onto the dusty streets of the intimidating city, you know you won't forget it.

Sam Predgen-Lay

Watching

I sit on the roof looking out on the
world, just watching.

Watching as the trees, silhouetted black
against a hazy crimson background, cast
long thin shadows across the grass.

Watching a perfect ball of swirling flame
sink below the horizon.

Watching the crimson of the sky bleeding
into dusky pinks and oranges.

Watching as the ever-fading light seeps
through the scattered cloud.

Watching the pinks and oranges fade into
deep violet waves of colour.

I watch as the dark blue sky is slowly
punctured by tiny pin pricks of light and
as the gleaming moon reveals itself from
behind a silver cloud.

Jess Ephgrave

Silver Chalice

The systematic, rhythmic mechanical beep of the metal
detector produced a high pitched whiny sound as it was
swung back and forth.
Eagerly it probed the ground below, searching for hidden
treasures. The pointy red needle on the screen remained
stubbornly at zero as its owner retraced his steps across
the same piece of earth.

He had been out in the freezing cold of winter for nearly
two hours and what had he found? Nothing, zero, zilch
and 'goose egg'.
He sighed with disappointment.
Obviously, this was a waste of time, he should have
known from the start that he would find nothing.

If he had listened to his senses he would be sitting in
front of a warm, cracking log fire inside the beautiful
drawing room of The Manor by the Lake.
But instead he was out here in the biting cold. He just
couldn't ignore that adventurous streak inside him that
whispered he might just find something.

He flicked his stone grey eyes towards the Manor house.
There was no denying it was an impressive building.
The archaic house was at least one hundred and fifty years
old. This was evident by the timeworn, weather-beaten
battleship grey stone walls.
The stain glasses windows depicted hundreds of scenarios
related to the house's history.

John loved admiring the multitude of colours in the
windows. Ranging from ruby red to lime green and sunset
orange.

A heavy but ornately carved oak door stood, underneath a
towering balcony, as the entrance to the house.

Entwined up the side of a wooden trellis that was mounted on the south facing wall of the Manor house, were several grey serpent-like vines, their colours reflecting the winter season.

John turned his eyes away from the Manor and refocused on the patch of lawn he had been scanning.
His feet suddenly stopped.
It was ludicrous to keep searching the same spot over and over again. He shut his eyes and listened to the little voice in the back of his head.
It was telling him to search down by the lakeside.
His eyes opened; maybe it wouldn't be such a bad idea.
His feet changed direction, heading towards the lake.

His leather brown walking boots caused the frosty grass to crunch and flatten beneath his feet as he trudged across, leaving distinct footprints behind him.
Then all of a sudden, the little red needle leant from zero towards three!
His pace quickened.
His eyes were glued to that red needle.
The beeping from the metal detector was becoming more insistent and frequent.

At last, the needle hit ten and the detector screamed one long endless beep!
John flicked the off switch and pulled out his trowel. He buried the steel point into the earth and began digging with furious intent.

As he dug, he wondered if he had found something valuable?
He doubted it.
He would probably end up digging up a water pipe... then he would be in trouble.
But something inside him told him that if he didn't try he wouldn't know.

He chuckled as he visualised his parents' reaction if he walked into their room with his arms laden with priceless treasures.
They, along with himself where spending the weekend at the hotel.
Something to do with his father's job, or so he had been told... Next, he turned his focus to what he would do if he found something valuable.

Probably sell it to some wealthy treasure hunter from Utah!
Then, he could give an agreeable portion of it to his parents, who would in turn use it to get the loft converted. He had lost count of the number of times they had discussed the idea... John's thoughts were rudely interrupted as his trowel connected with something metal!

John hurriedly began digging around the metal "something". It wasn't a pipe, thank God!

A good ten minutes later he had managed to unearth an iron casket.

John reached into the hole, his fingers wrapped around the cold metal handles and he tried to pull it from the ground.
It wouldn't budge.
Clearly the earth was unwilling to abandon its treasure.

John pulled harder.

The invisible tendrils of the earth still clung on to its prize, unwilling to share it with the rest of the world.

With an unexpected surge of strength that surprised him, he managed to free the chest from the ground!

He tumbled backwards with sudden force, generated
by the casket as the ground released it. John sat himself
up and brushed the dirt and soil off his maroon hoodie
before turning his attention to the chest.

The artwork on the chest caught his attention.
Dusty bronze squares circled around the middle like a belt
around the waist of a human.
Hundreds of intricately engraved, rusty silver roses
covered the dented lid of the strong box.
But most eye-catching of all where the four golden lions
that appeared to guard the latch that opened the chest.

Each one had tiny coal black eyes that appeared to watch
whoever was holding it.
Their perfectly carved manes inflated their already regal
presence on the chest.
The serrated daggers that were their teeth added a deadly
aspect to the lions' intimidating image.
He studied the condition of the chest.
Obviously it was very old and had been buried for
decades. John weighed it in the palms of his hands.
It was a good weight, there was definitely something inside!

His hands quaking with excitement, he flipped the corroded
latch up and he lifted the lid, the hinges creaking.
Inside the chest was a linen cloth-wrapped package.

His fingers, numb from the cold, fumbled to untie the
flimsy string holding the package together.

At last the cloth fell away.

John was glad he had listened to his adventurous streak
for in his hands now he held a silver chalice!

The winter sun glinted off its argentiferous body,
revealing all the different flower engravings.

There were three-headed thrifts surrounding budding
roses while spiky thistles coiled around the rim of the chalice.
John drew his index finger around the rim of the vessel,
where countless lords' and ladies' lips had drawn wine
from inside.
He flicked his fingernail against it; a metallic chime rang
out like a high pitched church bell.

John gazed at his discovery.
It was more than he could have ever asked for.
He carefully rewrapped the chalice in its cloth and
replaced it in its chest.

As he closed the lid, the casket let out a sorry creak.
He replaced the latch, put the chest under one arm and
picked up his metal detector with his free hand.
He couldn't wait to tell his parents about his discovery.

John quietly chortled to himself as he imagined the look
of envy that would appear on his younger teenaged
brothers' faces when they saw his find.

He had only taken four paces away from the casket's
secret grave when he remembered he hadn't replaced the
earth he had only a few minutes earlier so excitedly dug into.

His feet rotated on the spot as he turned to walk back to
the hole.
He had better fill it, in case someone fell in.

What a sight that would be!

And afterwards, he could brag about his silver chalice!

Jack McCune

64

On the Dark

Along the Road

Stumbling over the cobbles I very nearly
trip and fall.

The constant thought rages in my head,
"I have to get back to the house."

Noises behind me sound strangely like
hoofbeats and quicken to a sprint.
I venture to look behind for just a
moment, and see nothing.

So I stop to catch my breath, then turn
back to continue running and see a flash of
brown wood before the branch slams into
my head and it all goes black.

Alex Cassie

SLEEP

Silently lying there
In the dark room
Lying patiently waiting
Even when you lie awake
Even when you close your eyes
Peacefulness does not come
Sleep doesn't show its face

Silently lying there
In the dark room
Lying anxiously waiting

Even when you lie awake
Even when you close your eyes
Pleading for it to come
It will not show its face
Now you pace
Giving up your hope of sleep

Jess Ephgrave

Smoke

Amidst the dust and the smog of the city teeming
with factories and pollution where the wealthy care
not for the problems of the penniless, nestled in
the depths of one of the slums (of which there are
many), lies a cramped home.

This "house" is the dwelling of a small family who
cannot afford to live anywhere else.

The youngest in the family is a girl called Emma,
a five year old who lives with her mother
and two brothers.

Emma tries her best to be cheerful and optimistic,
even when things are hardest and always tries to
make her family happy

– which is easier said than done since her father died.

So she stays out of her family's way whenever she
can and wanders frequently about the slums
where she lives.

Alex Cassie

In Seconds

Pressing down on each piano key with
immense force, each hit of every key
producing a glorious tune when mixed
together to create a pure symphony.

That's where the incident happened.

In the midst of the captivating song is when
it happened.

Just as Evi was hitting the final notes to
complete the
mystical music, that's how it happened.

Her elbow carelessly knocked a glass of
water beside her.

With a yell, the water flooded the desk,
soaking through papers and staining the
letters until they were unreadable.

In seconds, everything had gone to hell.

Keisha Herbert-Valentine

Darker

In My Room

There's a Demon in my room.

Its charcoal black face is burned upon my shelf.

To the untrained eye and the unimaginative mind it is a
coffee stain, an odd pattern, but it's not,
it's a Demon.

Its face is a twisted black cloud, strangely shaped,
but a shape nevertheless.
Its eyes are wide and staring, as if it can see some
invisible horror.
Its mouth is open, aghast, unleashing a hellish
unheard scream.
I look at it sometimes and wonder how it got there.

Did an estranged carpenter put it in while making
the shelves?

Has the howling face been left on my shelves
as a joke?

Or, was it a real Demon that has been imprisoned on
my shelf by a noble hero or cunning wizard?

I don't know.

All I know is, there's a Demon in my room.

Jack McCune

Broken and Weak. Illustration by Lucy White.

Broken and Weak

Broken and weak,
the knife slipped out of my shaking hands.

The blood was caked under my fingernails, some had
reached the ends of my hair and it ran down the crevices
in my palms.

He had stopped breathing. His face was quickly turning grey.
The flow of blood from his chest was slowing down; the
puddle framing his body was growing still.

My cheeks were wet from tears but they kept my face
warm in the chilly night air.
My breathing quickened as I glanced at the dirty knife
lying at the edge of the red puddle.

I could see my blurry reflection in the metal. All I saw was
guilt and terror in my raw red eyes.

Trembling, my hands reached for the handle, and I started
to turn the sharp blade towards my chest.

The point dug into my skin.

I edged my back into the nearby railings, leaning my head
onto the freezing iron.
My breaths were rapid and painful: whimpers escaped my
lips with every fall of my chest.

My hands kept repositioning on the black handle, ignoring
my choice to end my life.

The knife was about to puncture my skin when I started
sobbing violently.

This should be an honour...to carry out my love's dying
wish. It was my only way out.

I could hear the screeching of a nearby car.

It stopped when its headlights lit up the corpse in front of me. The knife was becoming heavy and fell in my lap.

I could hear a car door slamming and wet footsteps on the road. I could barely look at my love's dormant face.
I was betraying him.
The driver was probably getting out their phone and punching out those three numbers.

A lifetime of living with criminals and bad food was ahead of me. I closed my eyes in acceptance.

I was a failure.

He was always stronger and braver than me.
A true believer.

My chin was about to drop on my chest, when I heard a click next to my left ear. A cold metal barrel had buried itself into my temple and my eyes flicked open.

It was one of them.

I thought they were all dead.

I was too scared and my throat too dry to scream.

The man chuckled.

       I gasped.
           Click.
               BANG.

Lucy White

Countdown

The watchers were filled with anticipation for what they knew was coming.

The grass was blowing in the breeze and the sun was shining; the air hummed with the throng of insects gathered around the flowers. The huge timer started the countdown...

10... the clock boomed as attention was drawn to the launch pad.

The watchers had been there all day, they wouldn't miss this...

9... the crowd chattered excitedly...

8... phones and cameras were taken out of bags...

7... food was put aside...

6... the humming of bugs continued...

5... words died on people's lips...

4... this event would be talked about for years...

3... a dog stole a forgotten sausage...

2... there was silence among the people...

1... a distant rumble and then a roar as the rocket left the ground, climbing slowly, then faster, leaving a fiery trail behind it as it arced away like a burning drill piercing the heavens.

Alex Cassie

Dark Smiles

There's a darkness in smiling.

Much like quicksand,
You can't test the land with your eyes.

You walk over it then you
suddenly start to sink.

Much like a dark smile,

That invites you,
Then breaks you with a shock
like a twist in your neck,
Your body is then buried with the rest.

And the other fools are reassured.

Smiles aren't harmful,

Unless you believe the plastic narrators
that flash their teeth at you,

Who wear lenses made of numbered paper.

True kindness does not want gold
for which you laboured.

The endless cycle of plastic and numbers
and gold that sucks people's souls,

And leaves them as robotic shells,

That have a thirst to consume,

And the dark smiles,

Who lead this army,

Of miserable, pathetic ants,

They'll all break down to nothing.

Just like the hoards of matter they
lock behind their names.

Lucy White

Into the Fire. Photograph by Freya Gray and Imogen Carter.

Into the Fire

Kane Jacobs was a revolutionary surgeon world renowned for his groundbreaking methods.

One dark December evening while driving home from a party with his wife, a truck slammed into their car causing shards of glass to fly into Katherine's face.

He crawled from under the wrecked vehicle and saw his wife lying motionless on a bed of glass and oil.

The next day, blaming himself, he burnt down the hospital he had worked at for 20 years.

He saw his flesh blister and burn, permanently disfiguring him.

He tied survivors to hospital beds and without anaesthetics tried to make them look

"perfect."

In his fleeting final moments of sanity, he used iron chains to restrict himself.

Louis Maxted

Joking Hazard

Office

My mum has an office just off from my bedroom.

The office can be described in many words.

Neat and tidy are not among those words.

She seems to be able to cope with it like that, but no one is quite sure how.

Mum often has trouble finding the things she wants in her office, but she always seems to find them eventually.

This ability to find what she is looking for is slightly suspicious...

Maybe she's simply good at finding things.

Maybe she's just lucky.

Or maybe there's more to it than that.

It could be that she has help.

It could be that there is a tiny civilisation in one of those cabinet piles of what she says is crafty things but I think is just junk.

The truth could be that she is some sort of witch using spells to find what she needs.

Alex Cassie

86

A Lesson in Trickery

My school, a wretched hive of scum and villainy.
When the bell tolls after lunch, it can mean only one
thing... the children of 7b are on their way to Mr
McMahon's maths class!

This was my position a mere four years ago; Mr
McMahon was a ruthless old creature, his nose was
as long as his temper was short.

To avoid his classes, myself and a close friend would
go straight to the toilets after lunch and sit in the
cubicles.

Waiting.

Waiting for the clock to strike three so we could
make our way home.

An hour spent in the cubicles every day.
A lot of planning went into not getting caught.

To get away with this trickery we would bribe a
friend to answer our name during the register or had
them say we were ill or at the dentist
- a timeless trick that worked well.

However, every few minutes we would hear the door
to the toilets swing open.

We would raise our legs from view under the cubical
door and keep quiet, often resulting in the slightest
noise causing us to wait, dead silent, crouched atop
the toilet seat, shaking in fear with goose bumps
quickly growing, only to find out it was the sound of
the radiator.

Being in neighbouring cubicles meant we could communicate via whisper or knocking out Morse code; the downside led to a ban on eating school meals before we did this lest a few spicy farts caused us to choke to death on our own toxic curry fumes.

It used to be three of us in the first few months.

But poor James, he... he was caught by Mr McMahon...

The old git slammed open his cubical and poked out his eyes with a B1 pencil.

Or he gave him a harsh detention.

I can't remember, it's been a while.

Louis Maxted

Twisted Proverbs (and one gag)

Fortune favours the lottery winner.

A good captain always goes down with
his ship... talk about career suicide.

A picture is worth a thousand words, or
better yet a thousand pounds.

If you can't beat them,
build a wall.

When the going gets tough,
the politicians start resigning.

There is no such thing as a free lunch, however there is the Tesco meal deal.

All work and no play sums up workaholics.

Late to bed and early to rise makes a man bad tempered, miserable and groggy.

If you don't have anything nice to say, write it down instead.

Jack of all trades, master of none... whoever wrote this proverb will shortly be hearing from my agent.

What goes around comes around
(said the boomerang).

If you can't take the heat, get a fan.

If knowledge is power,
I need a bigger generator.

Even Dr Who was confused by the
NHS application form.

All good things must come to an end, including this book...

Jack McCune

About Our Lead Authors

Alex Cassie

Hello, my name is Alex Cassie. Life is not much fun at the moment due to difficulties walking and other things, because of brain surgery. But I still love reading and sleeping! **Beyond Words** *has been fun and incredibly enjoyable. I've met some great people and developed some skills and my confidence.*

Jess Ephgrave

My name is Jess, I am 15 years old and I have been living with Chronic Fatigue Syndrome for just over three years. I also have Coeliac disease. For the past year I have been unable to attend school so I have been having lessons with GHES. I live in Cheltenham with my Mum, Dad and my younger sister and brother. It annoys me every day that my life is not going the way I thought it would, but I make the most of what I can do. I love reading, art, music and cooking. **Beyond Words** *has been an amazing opportunity. Since taking part I have started to really enjoy writing and writing just for enjoyment, which is something I never thought I would say.*

Louis Maxted

My name is Louis "The lion" Maxted (don't ask about the lion thing, it's a long story). I am 16 but because my birthday falls in April, I was 15 when I started **Beyond Words**. *I attend hospital education with GHES because of my struggles with anxiety and other mental illnesses. I have a lifelong passion for writing stories and hope to one day make it my career. When I'm not writing you can usually find me playing guitar, watching insane amounts of pro wrestling, listening to bands such as Metallica and Black Sabbath, playing video games and of course eating chocolate... usually all at the same time.*

Jack McCune

*My name is Jack McCune and I'm 16 years old. This is my second year with the **Beyond Words** project. I owe so much to the incredible team of people who have made this possible. After three years out of school, due to my period of illness, I found myself unable to enjoy many of my hobbies; reading and writing being the most drastically affected. But thanks to the wonderful people at the Gloucester Hospital Education Service and **Beyond Words**, I have been able to reconnect to my active imagination and I am once again expressing my ideas through my pen.*

Sam Predgen-Lay

My name is Samuel Predgen-Lay and I spend most of my time on my computer. When I'm not playing video games I'm most likely sleeping because of my Chronic Fatigue Syndrome (CFS). CFS causes you to be very tired 24/7 and it's mighty fun! (Warning: previous sentence contained mild sarcasm). I am currently unable to go to school so I have tutors sent to my house by the Hospital Education Service.

Lucy White

My name is Lucy and I'm with Hospital Education because of my M.E. I'm 14. I love my cat, anime, alternative rock and some classical music. As I've been getting better I've been drawing and teaching myself more piano. I collect art supplies. When I grow up, I haven't decided what I want to be – possibly a lawyer, or a journalist or an artist... or a director, composer or screenwriter. Even though I don't know precisely, I'm very ambitious and competitive, which is one reason why I really miss the school environment. But I'm going to start going part-time, which I'm really excited about.

Contributing Authors

Charlotte Lumsden

Lauren Arnold

Keisha Herbert-Valentine

Hannah Dingle

A word from a parent

It [**Beyond Words**] has taken Lucy to a place where she feels at home and comfortable and reminded her who she was before she became ill. She has rediscovered her creativity. She has loved this.

Caroline White, parent

Thank you to...

The **St James's Place Foundation** for kindly supporting the project.

ST. JAMES'S PLACE
FOUNDATION

The staff and management committee of the Gloucestershire Hospital Education Service for their enthusiastic commitment to **Beyond Words.**
Annalise Price-Thomas, Kathy Heathfield and **Ro Cole** from GHES for being an inspiration and a joy to work with.
The writer **Miranda Walker** for her dedication to the project and for her extraordinary ability to unlock creativity in the students.
Staff at Museum in the Park, Sudeley Castle, The Everyman Theatre and **Manor By The Lake** for their welcome and care in hosting the writing workshops.
The University of Gloucestershire Illustration Department for their support for **Beyond Words**, specifically to **Georgina Hounsome** and the many students who pitched their art work for the front cover.
The University of Gloucestershire Photography Department; to **Gemma Webb** and her students who created the photographs in response to the GHES students' writing.
Emma Evans at the University of Gloucestershire for designing and typesetting the anthology.
Rose Stuart for her meticulous copy-editing.
Chris Griffiths at StroudPrint for enabling the students to see their anthology being printed.
Waterstones in Cheltenham for hosting the Launch.

Most importantly we would like to thank the students and parents who have made this project such a success.

Your Turn

We would love this anthology to inspire you to write. Why not have a go at this story generating exercise that our writers enjoyed?

Building blocks exercise

What you need to know:

All stories centre on characters and dramatic ideas and (this next bit is important!) **drama equals conflict**. Without conflict, there's no drama, no dramatic tension, nothing very interesting happens in any story.
Inner conflict is one of the best sources of conflict for a writer to exploit.

Inner conflict arises from the inner feelings or beliefs that cause someone concern, stress, sadness, anger or disagreement. For instance, feelings of jealousy or low self-esteem, or a belief that they'll fail their exams or that they are cursed.

Feelings and beliefs will provoke certain behaviours, and these can inspire a whole story.

A **character** who feels jealous may sabotage a friend for example – a great dramatic starting point! A character with low self-esteem might avoid talking, which others could misinterpret as rudeness. That could really cause trouble with their boss, or head teacher, or the person they really fancy... you get the idea!

What you need to do:

1.   Create a character called Astrid. Think about the characteristics this name suggests to you and make a list. You might like to think about Astrid's personality (both flaws and attributes), age, attitude to life, occupation, hobbies and relationships. Remember those all important inner feelings too.
2.   Create a character called Jenson, following the same steps.

3.   Now think about how Astrid and Jenson could be connected to one another, or how they could meet. This should be informed by their character profiles. (E.g. if Astrid is 70 years of age and Jenson is 14, perhaps he's her grandson.)

4.   Next, think about conflict that could arise between the two characters, based on everything you know about them. (Perhaps Astrid thinks young people have too much freedom these days, and fun-loving Jenson thinks she's a killjoy.)

5.   Now place them in a situation that will make the most of that conflict. Really put them through the wringer! (E.g. Jenson could have to stay with Astrid for the whole summer holidays.)

6.   Once your story idea starts to come together, you can tweak and develop your characters, and eventually come up with the whole plot.
Hannah Dingle took part in this exercise. She thought Astrid sounded like a name from a fantasy book. This led her to come up with the following ideas for steps 1-5:

Astrid is a female fire fairy. She's a strong, monster-slaying character who wants to rid the world of evil, taking advice from no one. Fiercely beautiful with an aura that tells you that it's the things she has gone through that have made her so strong. The name Astrid means 'Godly strength and divine beauty.' This sums up her character well. She shoots a bow and arrow with near perfect precision.

Jensen is a man with a rugged look. He's had much life experience and loves rock and roll. He's caring towards others but never opens up to anyone... not since he lost his brother to a monster a few years back. A monster he needs to confront if he's to lay his own demons to rest. Jenson doesn't possess magic but is great with a sword.

Conflict:
Astrid and Jenson find they are hunting the same monster, but they have fiercely opposing views on how it should be cornered and dealt with. This doesn't stop Astrid from pressuring Jenson to join her and to fight. It's forbidden for a fairy and a 'non-magic' to have a relationship, but even as sparks fly and tempers blaze, there's no denying that something bigger than both of them keeps pulling them back together.

Hannah certainly has the makings of a dramatic story there.
I really hope you have a go too.

Happy writing!
Miranda